I0692627

James McKaye

Of the Birth and Death of Nations

A thought for the crisis - Vol. 2

James McKaye

Of the Birth and Death of Nations
A thought for the crisis - Vol. 2

ISBN/EAN: 9783337378608

Printed in Europe, USA, Canada, Australia, Japan

Cover: Foto ©Andreas Hilbeck / pixelio.de

More available books at **www.hansebooks.com**

OF THE

BIRTH AND DEATH

OF

NATIONS.

A THOUGHT FOR THE CRISIS.

NEW YORK:
G. P. PUTNAM, 532 BROADWAY.
1862.

BIRTH AND DEATH OF NATIONS.

IN the primitive ages of the world, long before the dawn of history, while Prometheus lay chained to the rock, and the men of Shinar, dispersed by the divine anger, settled themselves in new habitations, there was sent into that far off eastern country, the earliest home of the race, a messenger from the celestial powers. With a virgin's head and face, she had the stalwart body of a lion and the strong wings of an eagle. She had been taught by those primeval intelligences and instructors of the gods, the Muses, and knew all the wisdom of the ages, past and to come; and her commission was to stand on the waysides, and in the great thoroughfares of the people, and put questions—riddles—to the passers by. Questions, doubtless very apt, significant and necessary to be put, but often, to that infant race, most obscure, enigmatical, and difficult of right answer. And yet there was no escape; answered they must be, wisely, justly, and to the point, under penalty of a sudden and sure destruction,—for such was the inexorable decree of the inscrutable Powers that ruled that ancient world. To-day even, whoever likes and can afford it, may see her colossal image cut out of a black basaltic spur of the Libyan mountains, overlooking the Nile, a neighbor and meet companion of the great Pyramid of Cheops.

To the Greeks the SPHINX was the offspring of the Chimera. In disparagement of her authenticity, the sceptics call her a MYTH, as if the Myths were not the oldest and most indestructible facts in the history of the world. But by whatever name she may be called, from that remotest period of the ethnic formations of humanity, the beginnings of nations, even unto this day, have her arduous questions been propounded, and always with no jot or tittle of the old penalty abated—a right true answer or certain overwhelming ruin.

On no habitable summits of the earth, in any age of human history, have questions of a higher import or involving mightier interests, secular and eternal, been put to the sons of men, than those that to-day so urgently press themselves upon the consideration of the people of these United States. Nor can their just solution be any longer avoided or delayed, under forfeitures more disastrous and deplorable than any people ever before were called upon to pay. For this is the nineteenth century of the Christian era, and we live under its Master's unfailing word—"Unto whom much is given, much will be required." Very necessary is it then, that we should lift ourselves intelligently to the moral level of these questions, and in the faith that truth alone has the right to reign over the world and to govern its facts, without attempting to anticipate or forestall the final dispositions of the Infinite Providence, make our answer fearlessly, in the light of that WORD, and of history.

And first of all, in the order of events as well as of the argument, it is demanded of us to answer by what RIGHT we call ourselves a nation, and claim to hold and rule as one INDIVISIBLE DOMAIN, all these broad territories, stretching from ocean to ocean?

The question is asked upon quite another and higher authority than that of any Confederate States' president or congress. Nor does the roar of their cannon constitute the most urgent reason for its prompt answer. That became necessary only in consequence of the obdurate dulness of the national ear to "the still small voices." Even so has it been from the beginning—"the still small voices" once became inaudible, and the Supreme Powers must needs commission the loud and ever louder ones, even unto the roar of whole batteries of rifled cannon. Already at Sumter, Bull Run, and elsewhere have these batteries belched forth such a denial of the nation's right to national existence, as leaves no doubt of the internecine nature of the hatred that so vents itself, and demonstrates the imminency of the crisis that urges us to a thorough examination of the grounds upon which the great battle must be fought, in order that *our* batteries may be planted upon the immovable foundations laid by the fathers, and our cannon charged not alone with the elemental forces of carbonized saltpetre, but, consubstantial with these, with the far more invincible logic of that Divine Word which in the beginning became flesh in this nation, and will, in defiance of all the powers of darkness that assail it, have free course and be glorified in its history.

Let us, then, to begin with, clear our minds of that atheistical, impious, secession vagary—that a nation is a species of heterogeneous, accidental aggregation of men or of states, held together by a sort of "balance of interest treaty" or contract of copartnership, entered into for the purpose of establishing and carrying on the highly profitable business of stump oratory "for Buncombe," securing "the spoils of victory" in certain annual games of ballot-box stuffing, and breeding "colored chattels" for the shambles of king cotton. This notion of the essential nature and purposes of our national existence, has now for several years been entertained, and by many distinguished politicians and leaders of the people, with no little energy, reduced to practice in these United States,—with what effect begins to be apparent enough. No more false or fatal emanation from the bottomless pit ever lodged itself in the human understanding, and the necessity of dislodging it with the truth seems just now very urgent indeed, to the present writer.

The TRUTH being that, even in the most rigorous scientific definition of it, a NATION is an organized body, and by no means a mere aggregation of individual men or independent communities; and so, like every other organized[1] body, must from the very nature of things, incorporate its own distinctive organic force or Idea. Indeed, it is only in virtue of this distinctive organic idea, that it becomes a nation at all. To this merely formal statement of the truth, history, irradiated by the light of eighteen Christian centuries, adds a far sublimer derivation and broader scope. It declares, that in the great epochs of the world, the Omnipotent Providence confides to a chosen people the revelation of a great truth, a great regenerative IDEA ; and that from thenceforth, that idea becomes for that people the germ of its national life and civilization—its soul, without which it could no more be a nation, than the human body could be a man without the human soul. For in this more excellent sense, a nation is but a larger form of humanity, a grander Cosmos or receptacle of the Divine Presence in the world. And it is this Presence, this fundamental idea, which constitutes the real substance of the national life, and determines the legitimate character and course of the national development and civilization.

This presence of a divinely posited fundamental idea, as vital force in the ethical evolution and growth of nations, is the highest, grandest fact in the history of the race. The sublimest theme of the oldest Scriptures is this doctrine of the genesis of all things from the Spirit "moving upon the face of the deep." The first product being light, thought, idea—and then the idea emerging into articulate word, a FACT in time. Not only the solid earth, upon which to-day beats the heavy tramp of our armies, was so founded, but so were embodied and established all the several nations that have dwelt upon its surface, even unto that one whose " covenant of life " bears date on the fourth day of July, 1776, and contains these ever-memorable words, then first in the providential unfolding of the ages made audible to the ears of men :

" ALL MEN ARE CREATED EQUAL, ENDOWED BY THEIR

CREATOR WITH THE INALIENABLE RIGHTS OF LIFE, LIBERTY, AND THE PURSUIT OF HAPPINESS."

"America," said the great Earl of Chatham, in a memorable debate in the English House of Lords in 1770, "was settled upon ideas of liberty." By what Promethean struggle has every simplest truth, every human right, to get itself established on the earth! What a career had that English humanity to run from whence America sprung, before even the dimmest adumbration of human liberty could emerge into articulate expression, and obtain for itself some faint acknowledgment as natural human right; some dubious authority as the *Common Law!* And even now, it is only where that law prevails that any such liberty exists. For wherever the civil or Roman law is supreme, such liberty as it recognizes, exists only as a franchise, as founded in the idea of a grant from lord or sovereign to his subject; and the idea has proved itself stronger than all the might of the people. No number of French revolutions, not even a "reign of terror," has been able to prevail against it. Is it not necessary, then, to believe in the solidity and strength of ideas? The very fact is, that the whole interminable web of human history is woven, "upon the roaring loom of time," of nothing else but ideas.

Doubtless the words of the wise old statesman were most true: "America was indeed settled upon ideas of liberty," but not of liberty only. Ideas of a still broader scope and grander aim, wrought silently but strenuously in that settlement; ideas originating in the advent of the divine Manhood into the world, and the sublime transfigurations thereby effected in the status and history of the race; ideas of the equal dignity and worth of the common humanity, in its own spiritual substance, as the begotten of God, the bearer of his image, the continent of his presence in the world, and, by right of its own nativity, endowed with the faculty of "life, liberty, and the pursuit of happiness." In no merely pagan age, under no merely pagan development, could this idea have been evolved. All the previous ages of Hebrew and heathen longing and endeavor were necessary, doubtless, to the great gestation and the coming of that "fulness of time." But then, as a condition precedent, the highest, divinest man must have the humblest parentage, the lowest birthplace, most necessitous life, and most ignominious death. So much must become a fact of history, and to this fact must be conjoined the idea, not less a truth, that this humblest, most stricken man was a Divine Presence—the very Logos of God—the Light of the world. This, and eighteen hundred years besides, of human effort and travail, of human failure and divine grace, were required to rehabilitate human nature with its original divine right of sonship to God, and to evolve the great regenerative idea upon which America was founded, and in which lie enwombed the germ and vital forces of its whole national life, civilization, and well-being.

What less than this idea of the consubstantial equality of all men—of man in his own substance as man, without regard to the accidents of birth, fortune, education, or complexion—could have supplied a ground broad enough upon which to found a nationality, whose membership from the beginning was intended to embrace the outcasts and expatriated of all the other nations and races of men ; and to whom should be given a whole continent for work-field ?

The advocates of what is called conservatism in England, which means simply a blind perpetuity of "the dead past," seem just now to take heart and jubilate amazingly over what they call a "failure of the democratic experiment." The men who for eight hundred years have held the proceeds of the great robbery committed by the hordes of William the Conqueror, and the men who have cunningly filched and funded the profits of the labor of the English worker for the same time, may naturally enough rejoice over even a semblance of failure of a system founded in ideas of human equality, and the right of the humblest man to enjoy the benefits of his own labor. But let them be assured that, whatever may be the issue of the present struggle in this country, there is not the least ground for their jubilation. In the first place, the "disruption" upon which they rely has arisen wholly out of a practical repudiation of the ideas upon which our "democratic institutions" were founded, and by no means out of any inherent defect in these ideas. In the second place, if the conspirators of the South should succeed in making the disruption permanent, and in founding a State upon a system which accomplishes even a worse robbery of human rights than that upon which older aristocracies are founded, it will not in the least constitute a failure of "democratic institutions," but rather purify and reinvigorate them, giving them new scope, power, and dignity, in the face of which no such system could long endure.

The truth is, that the perpetual mutations and revolu-

tions that so convulse and afflict European society have
their source in the antagonisms arising out of the circum-
stantial, the accidental in human condition, and the overwhelming class interests, upon which that society is founded.
Only upon that which is in itself durable, only upon the
permanent element in human nature—the equal dignity and
worth of manhood in its own spiritual substance—can any
nationality or social polity be founded, which shall at once
be permanent in its own nature and admit of a free development in all of its conditions. This is the ground of
Christianity—the ground upon which God founds his own
government of the world—the ethical evolutions of his
own providence, and, as a great product of that providence, of our nationality and free democratic institutions.

And in this lies the answer to the question as to the
nature of that right, by which we are authorized to call
ourselves a nation. But no spiritual entity, no *Idea*, can be
maintained in the world without giving it a body—without
making it a fact. In no other way can the fundamental
idea of our nationality be maintained, but by organizing it
into our social institutions, manners, and laws—by making
it, in all its grand and beneficent meaning, the basis of the
actual state and condition of the whole nation. In this
consists the real life and unity of the nation—its life and
unity in its own essential substance. The ethnic formation,
the body of the nation, is the product of this fundamental
idea; and they only in whom the idea inheres, in whom
it *lives*, and by whom it is faithfully developed, are in fact
the nation.

Very important is it, at this conjuncture in our national

history, that all men should clearly comprehend the nature
of this life, and the nature of that by which it may be
fatally injured and subverted. By no amount of material
power, by no number of battalions, can it be seriously af-
fected or endangered, so long as the idea in which it sub-
sists is retained in full force and virtue to vivify the hearts
of the People. On the other hand, that which attacks,
weakens, and tends to obliterate this idea, is to be regarded
as the *implacable* enemy to whom no quarter can be given.
For as surely as the great oak of the forest begins to wither
and decay the moment it ceases to obey the vital forces
contained in the germ from whence it sprung—the moment
it ceases to *grow* in accordance with the law of its own
organic life—so surely does a people begin to fall into ruin
the moment it ceases to develop the fundamental idea of
its own nationality, to work out its own appropriate civilization and history.

Can there be any doubt, then, as to our supremest, most
sacred national obligations? What else from the beginning
had we to do, but faithfully to execute the great providential
trust confided to us, to make the broadest meaning of that
solemn Declaration, fact in our history? Was not this the
immutable condition of the covenant made by the fathers
with God and humanity, in virtue of which we became in-
vested with the *divine right* of nationality, and for the
faithful performance of which they solemnly pledged, not
only their own, but, as its representative head, "the life, the
fortune and sacred honor" of the nation?

Has that solemn pledge been kept? Have we as a
People fulfilled the conditions of that covenant of national

life? What, in truth, has been hitherto the purport of our
national endeavors? Not to speak here of the unparalleled
development of our material interests and our really great
achievements in whatever appertains thereto; not to speak
of the genuine, manly work performed with "axe and
plough and hammer," or of its appropriate reward, abun-
dant crops of "Indian corn, and cotton, and dollars"—with a
FREE PRESS, PULPIT, and BALLOT BOX—what have we really
done, up to this year of our Lord, 1861, toward the ac-
complishment of the great providential undertaking committed to our hands?

The ear of the ancient Inscrutable Questioner listens for a
right true answer; and however deeply the national brow
may be suffused with the blush of shame, a right true
answer is supremely necessary to the future safety and
well-being of the nation. And the TRUTH, coined into the
gentlest admissible terms, declares that to us as a people,
whatever else we may have done of good or left undone
of evil, belongs the *distinguished infamy* of having given
birth to the idea, and developed into an *institution*, a
scheme of human degradation in which a human soul is
held bereft, not only of all civil liberty and rights, but of all
its natural attributes—is held to be not a *person*, but a bit
of *property*—not to possess even a *human* life, but only that
of a *beast*, and as a beast is kept for breeding other beasts,
(often with white men for sires,) for the public markets of
the world; a scheme which rolls back the civilization of
two thousand years, blots out the central idea of Christianity, and reëstablishes a worse than pagan barbarism; and
all this in the face of the great announcement, made

eighteen centuries ago, of God's all-beneficent intention to redeem, emancipate, and glorify the *nature* of his offspring —*human* nature. For what other meaning is there in that divine assumption of this nature, in its humblest condition? what other significance in the bewildered history of these centuries?

A cruel system of servitude did indeed exist among the ancient nations. But its fundamental idea was the idea of *authority*—authority absolute and monstrous, but still of authority and not of *property*. In ancient Greece, where the slave had no political or civil rights, his quality as a human being, as a man, was respected. It was only in Rome, that ultimate flower of all pagan cupidity and rapine, where slavery existed on a scale so monstrous as almost to defy belief, that something like the American idea prevailed. But even in the Rome of the emperors, the manhood of the slave was not totally annihilated. The old pagan master regarded his *servi* rather as ministers to his comfort or luxury, than as the subjects of traffic or a source of revenue. "In the household of an opulent senator," says Gibbon, "might be found every profession, either liberal or mechanical. Youths of a promising genius were carefully instructed in the arts and sciences." And yet, God in history never taught any truth more clearly or more emphatically, than that Roman slavery was the great enemy by which that grandest fabric of pagan civilization, the Roman nationality and empire, was utterly overthrown and subverted.

As the primeval perfidy, the primal thought of evil, which culminated in the first revolt of arrogant selfishness and pride, had birth in the highest circles of created intelligences, so it would seem that only among a people founded upon ideas of liberty and the equal dignity and worth of manhood, could a scheme so atrocious as Southern slavery be brought forth. An archangel only, could become the father of lies. Only the *inner light* of a people to whom the divine Manhood had been revealed, could become such utter *darkness*.

A most strange and portentous result of national endeavor, in view of the point from whence the nation set forth upon its career, is this American slavery—this *institution* of human depravation. Nor does the gist of the great evil so much consist in the outrage committed against the civil rights of the slave, as that in his person, not only is an irretrievable offence perpetrated against human nature, against our common humanity, but such a fatal injury to the vital idea of our nationality and civilization, as, if persisted in, we may not even hope to survive. For if the TRUTH set forth in that solemn national Declaration shall not succeed in making all men free, then the *false* shall triumph in making all men slaves. This is the inexorable divine law, of which all human history is but the illustration. The great false pretence, which the nation still so insanely persists in—the great lie, it so shamelessly holds in its right hand—by a fatal law of accretion shall draw to them all other perfidies, until the national heart and consciousness shall become so darkened and depraved that no sense of truth, human or divine, no love or reverence for any human rights, liberty, or manhood shall remain, and the national life and history shall become a very " devils'

chaos instead of a God's cosmos." In the communities
where the malign and lying spirit of slavery has taken the
most complete possession of the understandings and hearts
of men, this transformation seems already to have taken
place. So utterly has all sense of the most sacred human
rights and obligations been extinguished, all fealty and
patriotism eaten out, as to make the most atrocious vil-
lanies appear like innocence, and treason against the grandest fabric of human liberty ever erected on earth, like the
noblest of civic virtues—nay more, like the most sacred
and divinely imposed duties. Says the Rev. Dr. Palmer
of New Orleans, a man of learning and thought, and a
great authority in these communities, "*The great providential trust to the South is to conserve and perpetuate the
institution of domestic slavery.* Let us take our stand on
the HIGHEST MORAL GROUND, *and proclaim to all the world
that we hold this trust from God. In defending it, to
the South is assigned the high position of defending before all nations, the cause of all religion and all truth.*"

What else is this, but the ravings of the madness
and dementation engendered by slavery? What must
be the condition of a people, whose seers and prophets
have become so profoundly unconscious of their own
utter demoralization? By a like process have perished
the most powerful and proudest nations of antiquity. And
so inevitably must this nation perish, unless it can be
awakened to its true peril and moved to expurgate and
cast out forever the insidious perfidy, the fatal lie that
corrupts and consumes its vitals. For let not these people
be deemed worse by nature, than others. It is but the

blind and malignant spirit of slavery that speaks with their tongue, and with their hands brandishes its weapons. Is this a spirit any longer to be paltered with? Ought we any longer to entertain its insidious, treacherous sophistries? If that were possible, could we afford even at the price of the restitution of the external unity of the nation, to lose the light and glory of its internal life—at the price of saving our national body, can we afford to barter away our national soul?

We stand then at this pass. We know from whence and upon what conditions we hold our right to national existence and well-being. We know, beyond a peradventure, the implacable enemy that seeks their destruction. We know even, that by a necessity of its own nature, it cannot do otherwise than destroy them utterly, unless itself be destroyed. What else, in fact, is that open treason to the external unity of the nation, that to-day with so much "pomp of circumstance" sets its battle in array, but the outward expression of the far more dangerous treason that now for many years has been building its intrenchments in the national heart and sapping the very foundations of the national civilization and strength? What else, but the necessary outbreak of that subtle and malign perfidy that for a generation has burrowed in the national understanding, spawning its lies and sowing them broadcast through the land, until now, like the dragon's teeth, they spring up armed men—traitors. Or, does any man not stone-blind, believe that if to-day the Union were to be restored, and with it the pernicious cause of its disruption placed again under the guarantees of the Constitution, the

nation would not thereby be set back, to begin the great
war over again, unless slavery had thus secured to itself the
mastery of the National Government? This is its supremest
necessity, and the instinct of this necessity, conjoined with a
conviction that the mastery of the National Government had
escaped from their hands, compelled the slave masters to
undertake disunion at all risks. On this point we have
done these men a kind of injustice. Slavery can no more
exist under a government of practical freedom, than liberty
can exist under a government mastered by slavery. It is
but the common exigency of every *legally established
human wrong.* To secure itself against the attacks of light
and truth, against the perpetual encroachments, "coercions"
of human progress, it must be master of the power that
makes the laws. Under whatever political system or form
of government, therefore, slavery shall hereafter be permitted to exist on this continent, whether in a Southern
confederacy or a restored Union, it will, it must, from a
necessity of its own self-preservation, be master of the
Government and national institutions, and through these,
of the national life, civilization, and history. There is then
no alternative for this nation; either its own original, divinely endowed life must be surrendered up, or it must
conquer and destroy its unappeasable enemy, slavery.

That the nation possesses the requisite *material power*
to make this conquest, is not generally questioned, at least
in the loyal States; to say nothing of the *perennial strength*
inherent in the great idea of our nationality, which still
abides with them, and day and night cries out for *its* right
to conquer in this war. The question about which men

seem to doubt, and our public functionaries hesitate, is, has the nation the right to use the means of conquest which it possesses? It is said the national Constitution forbids it; that, by some extraordinary metamorphosis, this great palladium of liberty has the power only to cover and protect slavery. If this were true, the decisive answer would be that the Constitution was made for man, and not man for the Constitution. But it is a great defamation of that justly to be revered instrument. In its own nature, as a form of *national* government, as the supreme law of the nation, it recognizes the nation's right of self-preservation, and to use all the means necessary to that end. It recognizes the existence of the present most atrocious war, waged by the nation's enemy, slavery, and authorizes the sovereignty which it creates, to clothe itself with the rights and powers, known and acknowledged by all civilized nations as the laws of war; and by which all States and communities, in a state of war, are bound, whether it be a national or a civil war. So that the powers of the National Government, administered in strictest conformity with the Constitution, are just so far enlarged by a state of war, as are all the powers conferred by the laws of war. To disregard these laws, and the powers which they confer in time of war, is just as unconstitutional, in the truest meaning and intent of that instrument, as it would be to exercise them in time of peace. Nor is it by any means a matter of mere option with those upon whom the people have devolved the duty of carrying into effect the rights and powers of *their* Government, whether or not these powers shall be exercised. On the contrary, by their official oaths, by all the most sacred obligations that can bind the consciences of men, they are bound to see to it, that, in the present exigency, the nation suffers no loss, loses no advantage, that might arise out of the exercise of these constitutional war powers.

Already has the judgment of the nation and of history been pronounced upon the dastardly excuse, " a want of constitutional power," for the failure to suppress the rebellion in its very inception. No reversal of that judgment is possible, so far as James Buchanan is concerned, whatever may be the issue of the present struggle. In the history of his country, in the memory of all the coming generations of men, his name while it lasts will stand associated with the most worthless of his race—will serve as a byword to illustrate the most utter destitution of all truth, valor, and manliness in high station, the most pitiful, perfidious, and cowardly official failure that ever disgraced human nature ; unless, indeed, he shall have the good fortune to be forgotten in the presence of some still more infamous official delinquency, that awaits future developments in the history of our public functionaries. For, leaving out of the question the maxims of the highest order of statesmanship, the briefest consideration of the laws of war and the powers thereby conferred upon the National Government will serve to demonstrate, that if the servants of the people, who have been intrusted with that sacred duty, fail to destroy the cause of the war and thereby save the life of the nation, a repetition of his excuse—" want of constitutional power"—will not avail to save them from still profounder depths of public execration and infamy.

It is by no means my purpose here to enter into any
general exposition of the laws of war, but only to indicate
a few general principles, and the nature of the powers conferred by these laws upon every form of government in a
state of actual war.

According to the highest authorities on the laws of nations, these rights and powers are derived from one single
principle—from the object of a just war, which is to *prevent*
or *punish* injury ; that is to say, *to obtain justice by force.*
"In order, therefore, that a belligerent power may be en-
titled to the benefits of these rights and powers, the war
that it wages must be *just*, and prosecuted for a just and
legitimate end. Thence, the end being lawful, he who has
the right to pursue the end, has the right to employ all the
means necessary for its attainment, provided only that
these means are not in themselves contrary to the laws
of nature."

"That is to say, since the object of a just war is to suppress injustice and compel justice, we have a right to put
in practice against our enemy every measure that will tend
to weaken or disable him from maintaining his injustice.
To this end, we are at liberty to choose any and all such
methods as we may deem most efficacious. We have thence
a right to deprive our enemy of the possession of every
thing which may augment his strength, and enable him to
make and carry on the war. And if that of which we have
a right to deprive our enemy can help us, we have a right
to convert it to our own use, or to destroy it, whenever
that is necessary to the main object, which is to disable our
enemy and destroy the cause of the war.

"And thence, ultimately, all other methods proving insufficient to conquer his resistance, we have a right to put our enemy to death. And this upon the simple ground, that if we were obliged to submit to his wrong, rather than hurt him, good men would inevitably become the prey of the wicked."

"Under the name of enemy is comprehended not only the first author of the war, but likewise all those who join, abet, or aid in the support of his cause. So also, as between belligerent powers actually at war, all rights, claims, and liabilities affect the whole body of the community, together with every one of its members."

At this moment, slavery having organized its powers into a regular form of government, with all the functions of sovereignty, and embodied and sent into the field a military force, if not equal to that of a first-class European power, formidable enough to hold in check the great army of the nation, it is difficult to comprehend what real advantage can possibly arise to the national cause in ignoring the fact, and conducting the great struggle on the theory, which seems to prevail in the Washington Cabinet, that the rebellion is but a temporary insurrection and not a civil war. To the rebels themselves and their concealed allies in the loyal States there inure great benefits from this theory. For while slavery is left free to hurl its deadly missiles at the nation's heart, the heart of the treason itself is covered and protected by the ægis of the Constitution. On the other hand if, in spite of all constitutional or legal quibbles, this is a *real* war—a civil war, then the rights and powers arising under the laws of war clearly belong to the

National Government, are indeed as truly within the purport of the Constitution, as if conferred by express provision, and in the words of our wisest statesman, JOHN QUINCY ADAMS, "*abundantly sufficient to hurl the institution into the gulf.*"

While slavery remained upon its own ground, obedient to the Constitution, a due regard for the requirements of that instrument might justly be held to bind the National Government from dealing with it, as in its own nature it deserved. But the moment it threw off its obligations to the Constitution, and set at defiance the authority of the nation, the question of its existence became wholly discharged of all constitutional prohibitions and restraints; and from thenceforth the National Government was imperatively bound to take possession of it as a national affair; to deal with it, as with any other question vitally affecting the national well-being, on its own merits, and dispose of it with an enlightened, fearless, and far-reaching statesmanship.

But what a bottomless slough of absurdities, are even honest men compelled to swelter in, when once they have put their hand in that of slavery, and allowed themselves to be led by it! It is said the rebels have indeed committed a great outrage upon the Constitution, but that that is no reason why the loyal people of the Union, and their Government, should do the same thing *by abolishing slavery, the Constitution containing no express provision giving them that power.* As if the Constitution *did contain* an express provision authorizing the blockade of Southern ports, or filling them up with stone-filled hulks—the burn-

ing of the rebel's dwellings, imprisoning and slaying his
white children, and sweeping his whole land with the besom
of destruction.   Only one act, it seems, imposed by the terrible necessities of war, is unconstitutional, and that is, a
destruction of its cause, Slavery! No wonder that the great
heart of the world swells with a suppressed shout of de-
rision at such acumen and statesmanship. WAR and its
laws alone, justify and make *constitutional* any of these
acts. And much more do they justify and command the
utter extinction of its acknowledged cause.

War has been justly termed the "scourge of God."
And regarding it from the grounds of the broadest Christian statesmanship, it may, indeed, be pronounced an evil
in itself, in its own nature, so enormous, as never to be jus-
tifiable except on the ground that the continued existence
of its cause is a still greater evil. I believe the universal
conscience of Christendom, if appealed to, would confirm
this position. To destroy the existence of the cause, is
then the only legitimate aim and end in the prosecution of
any war. It follows, that a war carried on for any other
purpose, or with any other intent than that of destroying
or removing its cause, is not only unjustifiable, but a great
mistake, or a great crime. Only on the ground that
slavery, the admitted cause of the present war, is such an
evil, and that the war is aimed at its extinction, can it be
justified before God and mankind.

The existence of an apparent doubt on this point in the
minds of the men, upon whom rests the momentous re-
sponsibility of conducting the war to its highest, grandest
issues; and their paltering hesitancy to carry it on, upon its

own basis, as war, and for the achievement of a great and just end, is the source of disheartening anxieties and doubts, that wound and stagger the popular confidence of the loyal States. Nor is this by any means its only mischief. It gives occasion for an undeserved defamation of Republican Institutions, and contempt of our national character and aims abroad, that threaten us with the loss of the respect of other nations, if not with their active hatred and hostility.

Nor, on another ground than any hitherto set forth, can this paramount question be any longer left to be trifled with, by epauletted officials, high or low, without peril to the supremacy of the civil power of the nation, and shame to the representatives of the people. The powers conferred by the laws of war, belong, primarily, to the supreme authority of the State, and by no means, without its authorization, to any one of its administrative or executive functionaries. The Constitution, itself, takes on these powers, and Congress is its proper organ for their distribution—for giving them practical authority. Besides the fact, that the legislative power is alone adequate to the determination of the great question, is alone adequate to foresee and provide for the future of the slave as well as of the nation, in the presence of the great military force called forth by the exigencies of the hour, to watch with a most jealous eye every attempt of its chiefs to overstep their function, as the arm and servant of the civil power, is a matter of the most urgent necessity, and a sacred duty of the people's representatives. Most calamitous and deplorable indeed would it be, if the war to restore the external

2

unity of the nation should end, not only in reinstating its cause, as a supreme power in the State, but in giving the people a military autocrasy for their free republican institutions. In a war carried on for the maintenance of authority only—for *empire*, merely, this is an evil consequence, greatly to be feared. On the other hand, let your battle be for a great IDEA—let your army be inspired by a great sentiment of human justice and liberty, and the danger is cut off at its very source.

But why should the people of the United States, or their Government, seek to shuffle off the "inevitable logic of events," or squander the providences of God? The conspirators against the life of the nation, plant themselves openly, squarely, on the ground of Slavery. The war they wage is trammelled by no mental or moral reservations, no ambiguity of purpose. To make slavery triumph on this continent, and to found upon it a social order and a State, is their loudly vaunted aim, in its prosecution. The malign spirit has taken complete possession of their souls; they believe in it, are terribly in earnest about it, ready to die for it! On the other side, on the part of the nation and its Government, what great purpose is set forth to justify, inspire, and sustain them, in the prosecution of so gigantic a struggle? Is it to restore the rebellious States to the Union, and slavery to the safeguards of the Constitution! To reëstablish the fatal, malignant evil, not only in all its original power, but from the very nature of things, to give it renewed strength and vigor!! For they fall into a most pernicious error who imagine, that in some accidental or fortuitous way, slavery is to receive its death wound in this

war, even although it may end in its reëstablishment. Let
no such monstrous delusion be entertained. The ethical
Providence of the world never returns upon its own foot-
steps. God wastes not a single one of his dispensations,
repeats not one of man's neglected opportunities. Slavery
must die, and die now, by the enlightened will of the nation, or the nation itself must die—must have its own
heart eaten out by its poisonous, deadly virus.

But without reference to this inevitable and final con-
summation, what a solecism in human affairs does this war
present, when viewed from its own ground, as war, in the
light of its own logic! In the history of the world, was it
ever before proposed to " conquer a peace " by carefully
maintaining the cause of the war ? Was it ever before proposed " *to weaken and disable* " a powerful enemy, by be-
coming the keeper, and enforcing the labor of four millions
of his subjects, for his sole benefit and support ? To "*overcome his resistance*" by compelling a supply of the very
means, without which he would become utterly helpless ?
Suppose, for an instant, that these four millions of unwilling
workers, from whose labor the enemy draws his daily sus-
tenance, were in a night to have the color of their skin
changed to the Caucasian hue, and these white men were
to send a message to the Commander-in-chief of our armies,
that they were loyal men, lovers of liberty and the Union,
and only awaited his permission to rise in their might and
with one fell swoop destroy the cause of the war, and the
malignant power of the enemy. And suppose that this
Commander-in-chief should refuse the proffered assistance,
and insist that his *constitutional* duty was, to employ his

great army in standing guard over these willing allies of
the nation, and in compelling them to serve, and support
its implacable enemy. What judgment would a skilful
strategist, an able general pass on such a plan for carrying
on a great war? What would be the sentence of the
nation and of mankind on such patriotism and statesmanship? And yet, is not this a sober statement of the facts,
as they present themselves at this moment, with this
difference only—that the men, who, the other day, with
cries of joy, ran to embrace our army on the shores of Port
Royal while its enemy fled, had not all cuticles of the
supposed color?

By what unparalleled infatuation is it, that even yet,
after all the overwhelming proofs of the execrable character of slavery, the understandings and hearts of our public
men are enthralled and awed in its presence—bound abjectly, as by a spell of Circé, to cringe and bow to its dia-
bolical intimations. Under the pressure of the great exigency created by it, our rulers have not hesitated to set
aside the most sacred rights guaranteed by the Constitution. In the name of national safety they have not hesitated to suspend the great writ of freedom, the *habeas
corpus*, for two hundred years held sacred by all men
speaking the English tongue, and to put manacles on the
hands of American citizens. But to refuse any longer
to stand guard over the rebel's slave, or in the name of
liberty, the rights of human nature and of national existence,
to permit his shackles to be knocked off, is a thing only to
be thought of with fear and trembling—to be excused by
all sorts of phrases, and to be waited for, until it gets *itself*

transacted in some way, not to excite the latent treason of the half-suppressed rebels of the Border States, who, in the name of the old master, slavery, and with the old insolence, are still permitted to dictate the policy of the National Government, and give the word of command to the national armies. While the earnest convictions of the loyal people of the Free States, who furnish these armies, are flouted as fanatical and not to be regarded, on the ground, apparently, that their patriotism and love of country are unconditional.

Is it not time, O men of America, rightful heirs of the great inheritance, that we should rouse ourselves to a sense of the true nature of the enemy we have to overcome, and of the deadly perils that environ us? Look, I beseech you, at the battle-field, upon which we are called to pour out the blood of our sons—for who of us has not there a dear son?—what a spectacle does it present! On the one hand stands the great army of slavery, openly, boldly, proudly, in the name of SLAVERY, warring for its triumph. On the other hand stands the army of freedom, covertly, abjectly, in the name of *Union*, waging " a vague and aimless fight," but still for SLAVERY ! !

> " One guards through love its ghastly throne,
> And one through fear to reverence grown."

How, think you, must such a battle end? Shall not slavery, that " dares and dares and dares," not rather triumph, than liberty that cowers and hides herself? Or, rather, shall not liberty disown the cowardly, craven souls, that dare not fight openly in her name, and yield them up

to become, in very fact, the "mudsills" of that hideous
throne they so reverence?

We may not flatter ourselves: on this plan of the battle we need not hope to conquer. The inestimable sacri-
fices we offer will be but vain oblations. To the Eternal
Justice there is no sweet savor in them. O friends, we
must not allow our children to be so driven "like dumb
cattle" to the shambles. Let us demand an open fight on
the ground of the great declaration: "ALL MEN ARE CRE-
ATED EQUAL—ENDOWED BY THEIR CREATOR WITH THE IN-
ALIENABLE RIGHTS OF LIFE, LIBERTY, AND THE PURSUIT OF
HAPPINESS." Only in the strength of the great idea which
it contains, have we the right even to ask to conquer.
Only in its name dare we send forth our brave sons to die.
Only with the consolation that they fell in the cause of liberty and the rights of humanity, shall we be able to as-
suage the griefs that must wring and break our hearts
at their loss.

And you, ELECT of the people, who but now so eagerly
persuaded them that *you* were the qualified of God, and
fit to keep watch and ward at the doors of that CAPITOL,
the chosen temple of liberty and the rights of humanity on
this continent—is it not time that you should lift your-
selves to the level of the great issue? In the ethical
evolutions of our national history, a second great ERA pre-
sents itself—another "time to try men's souls" stands
face to face with the present hour. The question is not
now, as a high official personage seems to think, a merely
technical, attorney one, of construing the letter of the Constitution, but of refounding the nation, and rehabilitating

the national institutions and Government. Slavery by its own act has outlawed itself. The determination of its future status settles the whole matter in issue. To restore it now to the Union—to receive it again under the guarantees of the Constitution, would be nothing less than to refound the nation upon it—to make it the basis of our national institutions and the corner-stone of our future civilization and history. This calamitous consequence is of the very nature of things, and can by no means be evaded when once the ignominious restitution shall have been accomplished.

Besides, who, except those "that have eyes and see not," can fail to understand the providential intimation. These colored men of the South are the men whose blood should pay the price of their own redemption. If, in the present supreme hour, "there can be no salvation without the shedding of blood," they also should have the privilege of making the great sacrifice. It is the needed discipline and necessary preparation for the possession of freedom, that they who seek it, should be willing to die for it. It is for you to give them the opportunity—to organize and guide them into the ways of civilized warfare, instead of leaving them to grow into an irrepressible mass of barbarism, by and by to burst into a wild and all-devouring conflagration. For the sake of our common humanity, it is your most sacred duty to take possession of their destiny, bound up as it is with that of the nation, and, by your wisdom and foresight, guide them on *their* road to freedom, and *ours* to national regeneration and glory.

Hitherto, we have been able to answer to the re-

proaches of our fellow-men, on account of slavery, that its
existence ante-dated the existence of the nation, and that it
was but an extraneous incident in its history, for which the
founders were not responsible. But if now it shall be vol-
untarily taken back into the bosom of the nation, we shall
deserve, as we shall most surely receive, the open scorn of
all mankind.

But why should we not, in this imminent crisis of our
national existence, lay to heart the great lesson of the ages
—that the eternal Providence, that shapes all human will
and effort into history, even from a necessity of its own nature, cannot do otherwise than pursue, with an unappeasable divine hostility, all false pretences and lies—cannot do
otherwise than blast, with a celestial, eternal hatred, the
grandest human structures attempted on such foundations
—sending false nations as easily as false men to judgment
and eternal doom.

Many centuries ago, in another far-off land, a favored
people stood, like us, in the very pitch of a great national
crisis. The all-beneficent Providence had presented to
them, likewise, the opportunity of refounding their nationality upon a basis of eternal truth—that "truth whereby
all men are made free." The *final* question was put to
them with the same terrible emphasis that to-day it is put
to us: "Whom will YE have, *Barabbas* or JESUS called
the Christ." "Not He," they cried, "but Barabbas.
Away with him to the cross; Barabbas is our man—give
us Barabbas." And they got Barabbas, and with him such
guidance as a thief and a liar had to give. We know the
result. A nation for whom the *Deka Logoi* had been writ-

ten by God's own finger—who had stood at the nether part of the mount and seen with their own eyes "that God answered with a voice;"—a people who had Abraham to their father, and a long line of divinely-inspired men for teachers and guides; after eighteen hundred years of perpetual dispersion and dilapidation, from the hour of that fatal choice, are now, it is said, "prophetically crying ' old clo', old clo',' in all the cities of the world."

And to-day, even in this very hour, in all the thoroughfares of the people, upon the very threshold of that capitol where you, their ELECT, deliberate to become more renowned than any Roman Senate, or to sink into ignominious contempt and forgetfulness, stands the old Inexorable Questioner, and demands a right true answer to the *final*, *fateful* question, "Whom will *ye* serve, *slavery* or FREEDOM?"

www.ingramcontent.com/pod-product-compliance
Lightning Source LLC
Chambersburg PA
CBHW030915260626
47169CB00008B/2862